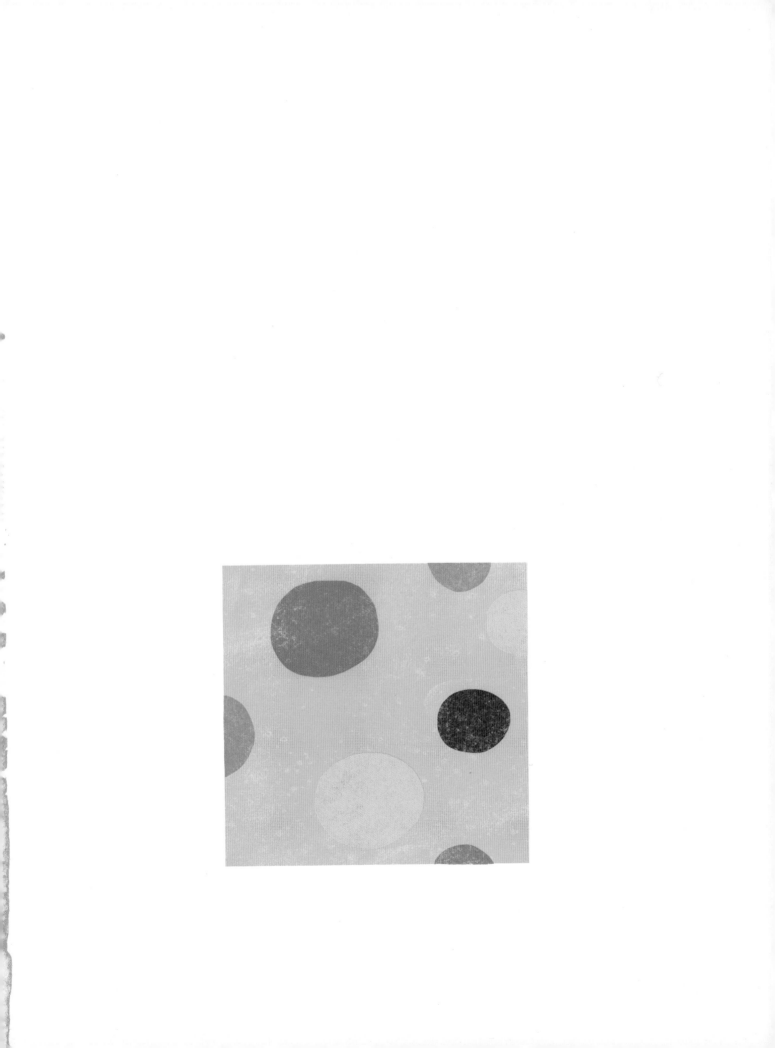

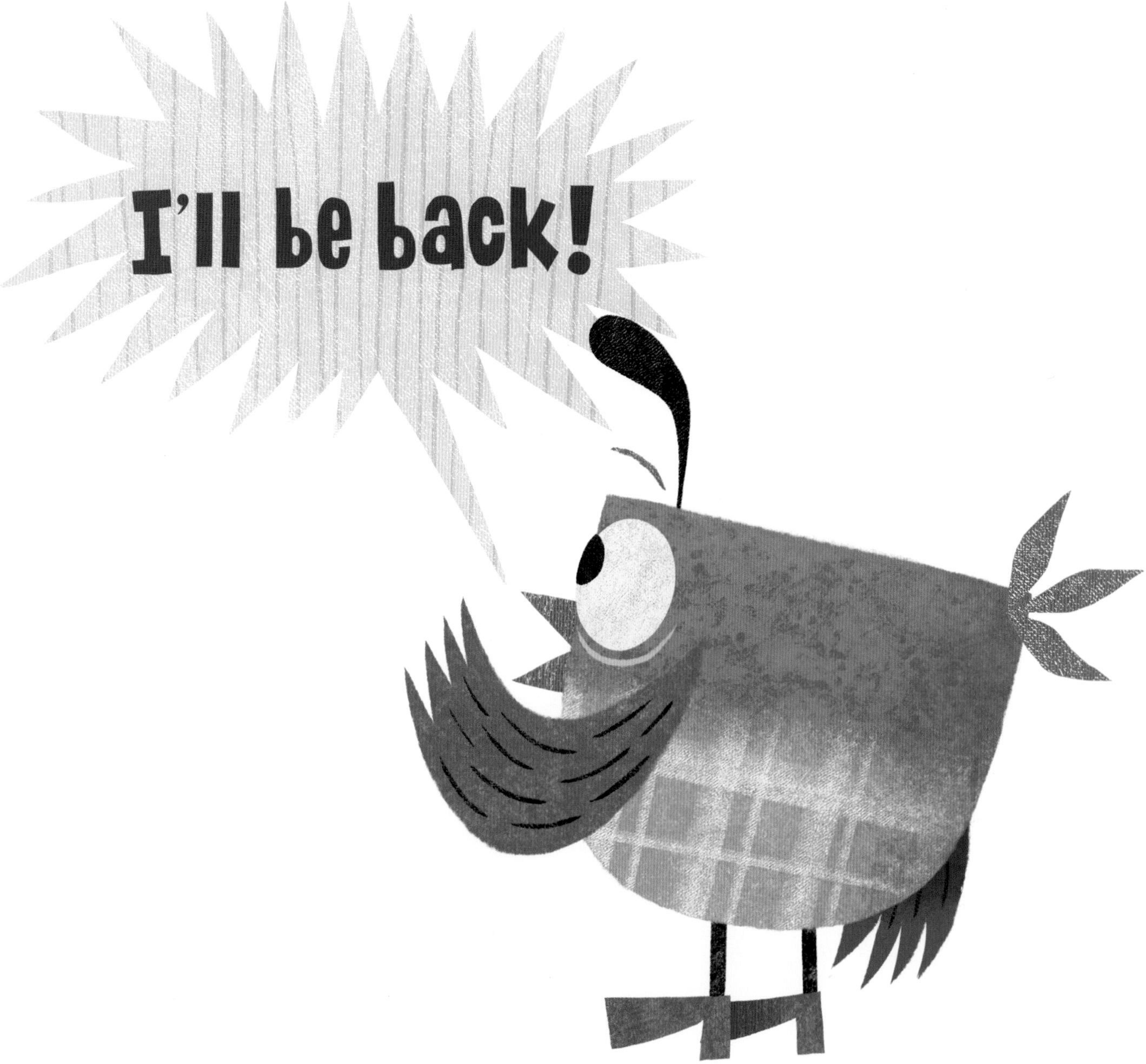
I'll be back!

SHORTY & CLEM

Michael Slack

HARPER

An Imprint of HarperCollins Publishers

Shorty & Clem
Copyright © 2017 by Michael Slack
All rights reserved. Manufactured in China.
No part of this book may be used or reproduced in any manner
whatsoever without written permission except in the case of brief
quotations embodied in critical articles and reviews. For information
address HarperCollins Children's Books, a division of HarperCollins
Publishers, 195 Broadway, New York, NY 10007.
www.harpercollinschildrens.com

ISBN 978-0-06-242158-6

The artist used Photoshop to create the digital
illustrations for this book.
16 17 18 19 20   SCP   10 9 8 7 6 5 4 3 2 1
❖
First Edition

For Clarence Locke.
My mentor and path pointer.

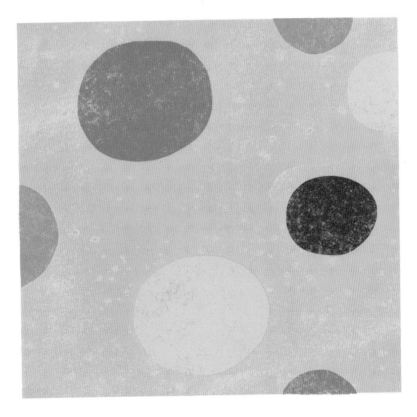

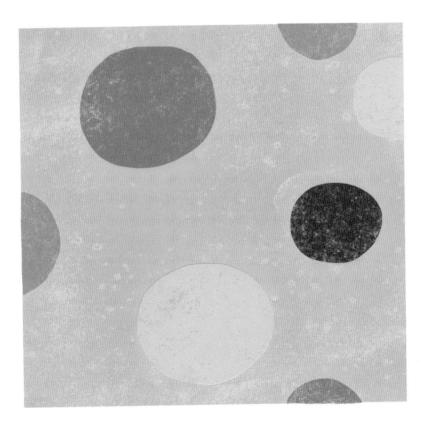

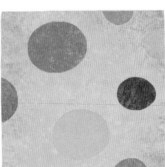

maybe there is a race car inside.

NO, this is not mine and I should not open it, but...

There you are. What's wrong?

There was a package for you and ...

SNIFF SNIFF

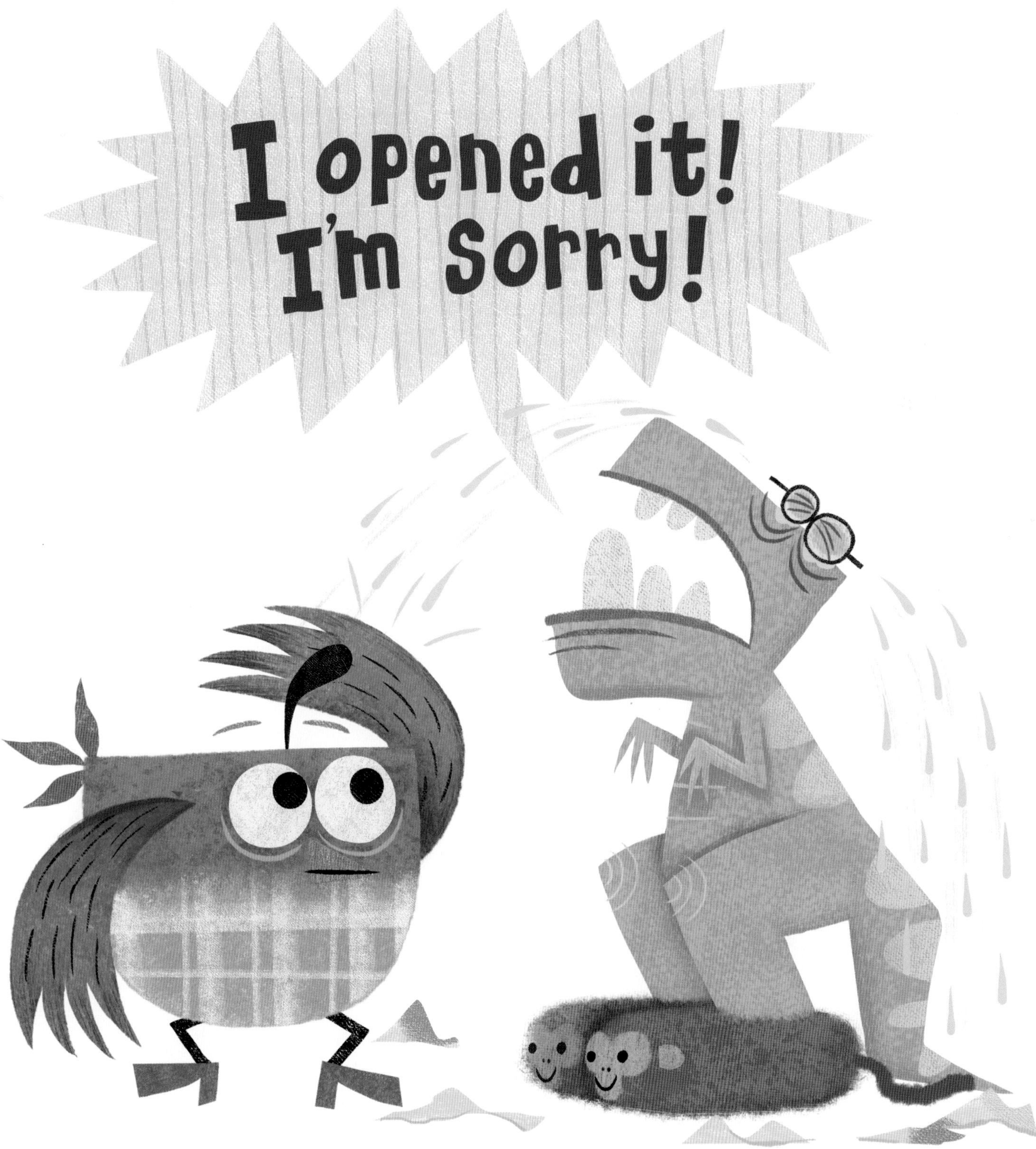
I opened it! I'm Sorry!

You opened my package?

A package addressed to me? With my name on it?

Were those in my Package?

I just have one thing to say!